To Elin —K.G.

Oi Evan! Oi Olivia!
My biggest *Oi Frog!* fans
— J.F.

Dog on a Frog? was originally published
in the UK by Hodder Children's Books,
a division of Hachette Children's
Books, under the title *Oi Dog!*

ISBN 978-1-338-22765-9

10 9 8 7 6 5 4 3 2 1   17 18 19 20 21

Printed in the U.S.A.   40

First printing 2017

The text and display type were
set in Coventry ITC Medium.

Book design by
Jennifer Stephenson

DOG ON A FROG?

By
Kes & Claire Gray

Illustrated by
Jim Field

SCHOLASTIC INC.

HEY, DOG!
GET OFF THE FROG

said the frog.

"But I like sitting on frogs," said the dog.

"Frogs are all **squishy** and **squashy** and when you sit on them they go CROOOOOOAAAAAK!"

"You know the rules," said the cat.

"Cats sit on mats, frogs sit on logs, and dogs sit on FROGS!"

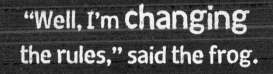

"Well, I'm **changing** the rules," said the frog.

"From now on, **dogs** sit on **logs**, not **frogs!**"

"REALLY?"
said the dog.

"REALLY,"
said the frog.

"Dogs sit on logs,

and cats sit on gnats."

"OUCH!"

"What will **bears** sit on?"
asked the dog.

"**Bears** will sit on **stairs**,"
said the frog.

"What will **slugs** sit on?"
asked the dog.

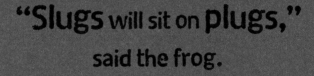

"**Slugs** will sit on **plugs**,"
said the frog.

"**Slugs** will sit on **plugs**,
flies will sit on **pies**,

crickets will sit on **tickets**,

and **moths** will sit on **cloths**."

"What will
leopards sit on?"
asked the dog.

"**Leopards**
will sit on
shepherds,"
said the frog.

"**Leopards**
will sit on
shepherds
and
cheetahs
will sit on
fajitas."

"You're really getting
the hang of this,"
said the dog.

"I know,"
said the frog.
"And that's
not all . . .

Gnus will sit on **canoes**,
pigs will sit on **wigs**,
and **boars**
will sit on **oars**."

"What will **whales** sit on?" asked the dog.

"**Whales** will sit on **nails**," said the frog.

"I'm not sure the **whales** will like that," said the dog.

"They don't have to like it," said the frog.
"They just have to do it."

"What will **dragons** sit on?" asked the dog.

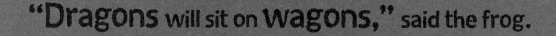

"**Dragons** will sit on **wagons**," said the frog.

"Dragons will sit on wagons,

mice will sit on ice,

kittens will sit on mittens,

and puppies will sit on guppies."

"What will **canaries** sit on?" asked the dog.

"**Canaries** will sit on **fairies**," said the frog.

"**Canaries** will sit on **fairies**,

possums will sit on **blossoms**,

hens will sit on **pens**,

baboons
will sit on
balloons,
and
poodles
will sit on
noodles."

"Poodles
aren't going to sit on
noodles!"
gasped the dog.

"They are now."
The frog smiled.

"Hold on," said the cat. "If dogs sit on logs,

and cats sit on gnats, bears sit on stairs,

slugs sit on plugs, flies sit on pies,

crickets sit on tickets, moths sit on cloths,

leopards sit on shepherds,

cheetahs sit on fajitas,

gnus sit on canoes,

pigs sit on wigs,

boars sit on oars,

whales sit on nails,

dragons sit on wagons,

mice sit on ice,

kittens sit on mittens,

puppies sit on guppies,

canaries sit on fairies,

possums sit on blossoms,

hens sit on pens,

baboons sit on balloons,

and poodles sit on noodles . . ."

WHAT ARE FROGS GOING TO SIT ON?

asked the dog.